# GO AWAY,
# UNICORN!
## DOGGONE MAGIC!

# For my parents

❧

Text and illustrations copyright © 2020 by Emily Mullock

All rights reserved. Published by Scholastic Inc., *Publishers since 1920*. SCHOLASTIC and associated logos are trademarks and/or registered trademarks of Scholastic Inc.

The publisher does not have any control over and does not assume any responsibility for author or third-party websites or their content.

ISBN 978-1-338-71600-9

10 9 8 7 6 5 4 3 2 1        20 21 22 23 24

Printed in the U.S.A.     40
This edition first printing, September 2020

Book design by Mauve Pagé and Veronica Mang
Packaged by McKellar & Martin Publishing Group Ltd.

# GO AWAY, UNICORN!

## DOGGONE MAGIC!

*Text & illustrations by*
EMILY MULLOCK

SCHOLASTIC INC.

**M**ax was a dog with a happy life. He loved his perfect home, his family, and his Alice. Everything was perfect.

Then Unicorn came along and ruined everything.

Unicorn had come looking for birthday cake. He stayed because he knew that he and Alice were going to be best friends. And unicorns can be very persistent.

Unicorn was here to stay. He bedazzled Max's favorite sweater. He popped Max's squeaky toy with his horn. And he drooled all over Max's Barky Bites.

And Max loved his Barky Bites.

**B**efore Unicorn...

Max helped Benny get his ball.
He played "Let Go, Max!" with Dad,
and he ate delicious can-shaped
food thanks to Mom.

Best of all was Alice. She always
had time for Max, especially when
he was afraid. Alice scratched Max
in all the best places. And Max
loved scratchies.

**B**ut now there was no time
for scratchies. Alice was
always busy.

She baked rainbow cookies with
Unicorn, made rainbow crafts
with Unicorn, and took time
to explain to Unicorn how much
she didn't particularly care
for rainbows.

No one asked Max if he liked
rainbows. And Max *loved* rainbows.

There was no time for walkies, or Barky Bites, or tummy patsies, or anything else. Everyone was having too much fun with Unicorn.

Max had a serious problem.

It's a well-known fact that dogs solve problems better on a full stomach.

**M**ax munched and munched. He needed a solution to Unicorn's magical menace.

Max was very distracted by snacks. It took him a minute to realize something strange was happening.

He was glowing and floating far above the ground!

A nd Max realized that he
really, really loved the ground.

**B**ut there was an unexpected upside to floating. Everyone was paying attention to Max. Even Unicorn was impressed. Unicorns know a cool light show when they see one.

Only Alice was concerned. She liked Max the way he was. So Alice and Unicorn launched an investigation.

Magical Max was a big hit. He dusted the highest shelves, he made the perfect night-light, and he turned walkies into "fly-ies."

Still, Alice and Unicorn didn't seem to notice. They were busier than ever with some secret project.

It seemed not even magic could bring Alice back. There was only one thing to do.

Almost everyone knows that dogs sulk better on a full stomach.

**M**ax munched away. He was so distracted he didn't notice he was glowing brighter and brighter. Until he accidentally created an indoor ... THUNDERSTORM.

Max did *not* love thunderstorms. Everyone ran for cover. Alice's family was used to magic, but no one knew quite what to do about a thunderstorm *in the house.*

Except Alice.

Alice knew how to calm a frightened Max.

She ignored the storm and walked right up to Max. She scratched him in all the best places. They were the best scratchies he'd gotten in a very long time.

The storm faded away.

At last, Alice and Unicorn revealed their secret project—"The Case of Magical Max." They'd been trying to help the whole time!

"It's easy to confuse Rainbow Bitz for Barky Bites when you're upset," said Alice. Everyone agreed to make more time for Max.

Max was relieved to know he'd soon be back to normal. He loved his family (even Unicorn), and never wanted to mess with magic again.

But unicorns know that a little magic can be very uplifting.

And Max decided that one more pet in the family wouldn't totally ruin things. At least for now...

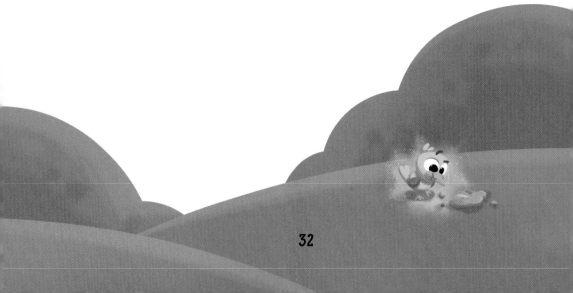